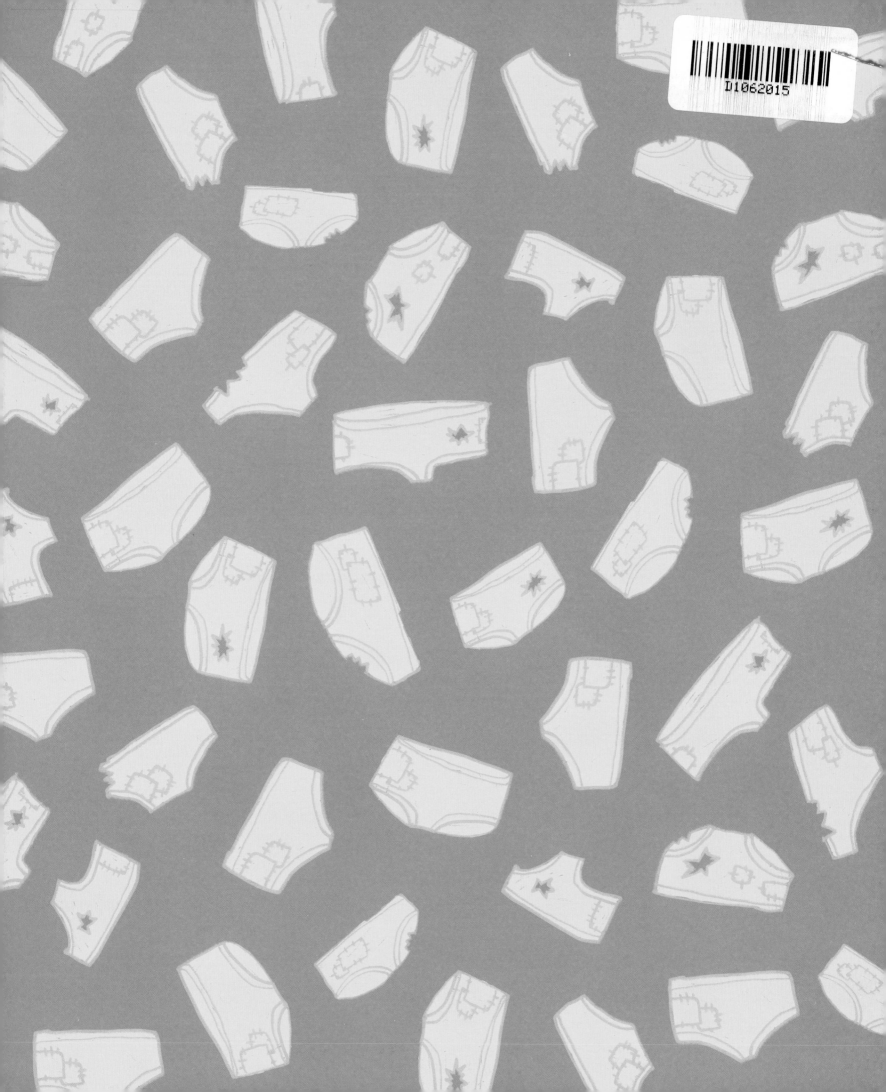

To Rami, when I'm by his side
I'm never afraid and I'm always laughing.

José Carlos Andrés

To Sergio.

Gómez

The Ghost with the Smelly Old Underwear
Somos8 Series

© Text: José Carlos Andrés, 2021
© Illustrations: Gómez, 2021
© Edition: NubeOcho, 2022
www.nubeocho.com · hello@nubeocho.com

Original Title: *El fantasma de las bragas rotas*
English Translation: Cecilia Ross

Text Editing: Caroline Dookie, Rebecca Packard

First Edition: January, 2022
ISBN: 978-84-18599-43-9
Legal Deposit: M-27411-2021

Printed in Portugal.

The GHOST with the SMELLY OLD UNDERWEAR

José Carlos Andrés

Gómez

nubeOCHO

Everyone in
SCARYVILLE lived in fear.

Why did everyone in Scaryville
LIVE IN FEAR,
you may ask?

Because there lived…

THE GHOST WITH THE SMELLY OLD UNDERWEAR!!!

He appeared when the townspeople went to the movies…
"I'm the ghost with THE SMELLY OLD UNDERWEAR. BEWAAARE!"

And often at dinnertime… "I'm the ghost with
THE SMELLY OLD UNDERWEAR. BEWAAARE!"

At times he even appeared at the garbage dump! "I'm the ghost with **THE SMELLY OLD UNDERWEAR. BEWAAARE!**"

Everyone in Scaryville was tired of **BEING FRIGHTENED ALL THE TIME.** They called a town meeting and asked for a volunteer, someone who could march up to the castle and tell that ghost once and for all,

"KNOCK IT OFF!"

MR. REDPEN, the schoolteacher, offered to go.
"I'm not afraid of anything!"

He stepped confidently onto **THE DRAWBRIDGE** and entered the castle, singing to himself as he went. "Everybody grab a pen and write a song for your hen!"

But JUST THEN—

"I'm the ghost with **THE SMELLY OLD UNDERWEAR. BEWAAARE!**"

"AHHHH!"

And with that, Mr. Redpen jumped promptly into the moat.

Since Mr. Redpen was still recovering from the scare,
the townspeople sent **SHIRLEY THE BURLY** instead.

But as soon as Shirley set foot
inside the castle…

"I'm the ghost with **THE SMELLY OLD UNDERWEAR. BEWAAARE!**"

"Eeek!
I want to go to the TOILET!!!

Then the townspeople sent in **MS. PITER THE FIREFIGHTER.** She took her helmet, a long hose, and an enormous ladder with her.

She climbed to the ROOF… Then she placed her ladder
inside the chimney and started climbing down
and down, until suddenly—

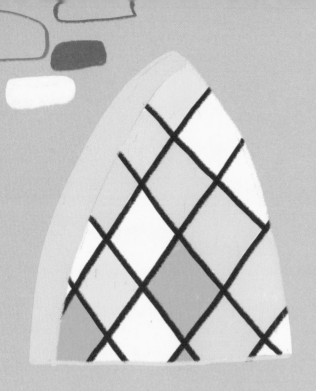

"I'm the ghost with **THE SMELLY OLD UNDERWEAR. BEWAAARE!**"

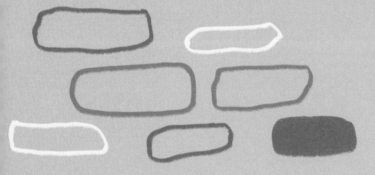

And with that, Ms. Piter the Firefighter
froze stiff with fear and waddled away **LIKE A PENGUIN.**

Finally, **OLD GRANNY FANNY** rose to her feet.
She picked up her purse and made her way slowly to the castle.

She knocked on the door once… twice… three times.

No one answered, but it wasn't locked,
so she stepped inside.

"Hello? Hellooo?? **HEEELLOOO?!?!"**

Just then…

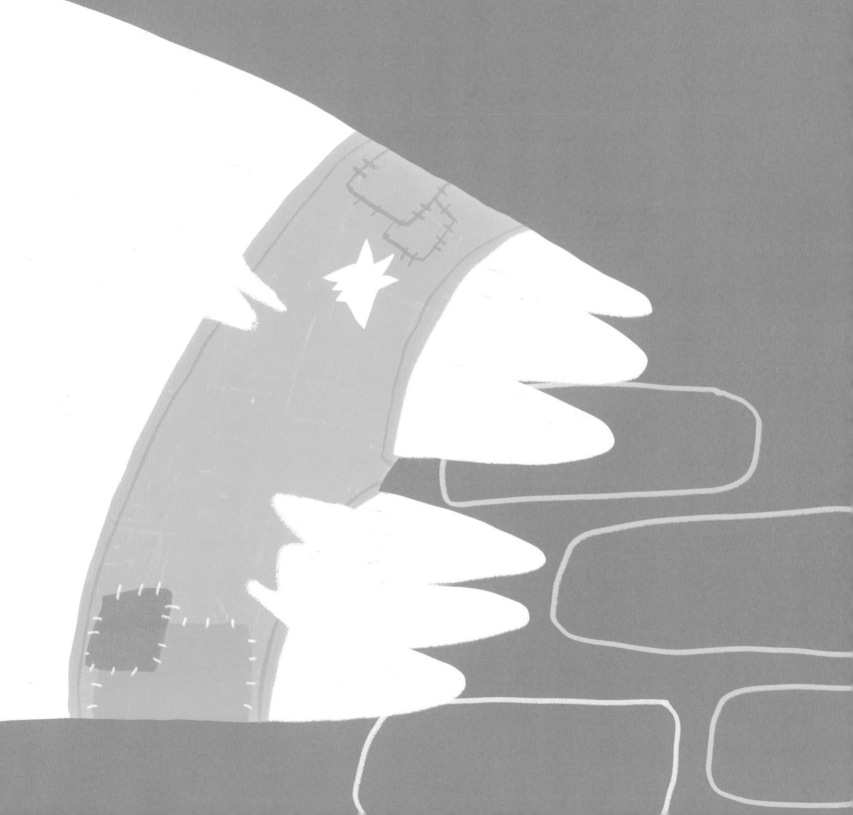

I'M THE GHOST WITH
THE SMELLY OLD UNDERWEAR.
BEWAAARE!!!

"The ghost with the smelly old underwear, you say?"

"Then put on **SOME CLEAN ONES RIGHT AWAY!**"

When the Ghost saw the clean new pair,
it burst INTO HAPPY TEARS...

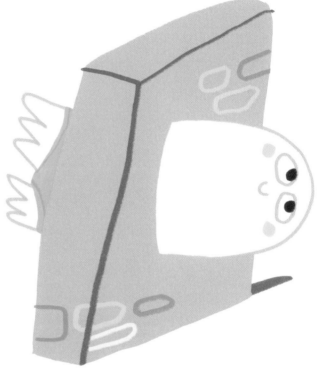

floated through THE WALLS...

and gave
Granny Fanny four
GIGANTIC KISSES.

A few days later, Old Granny Fanny and the Ghost **TOOK A STROLL TOGETHER,** greeting all the townspeople as they went. Some people greeted them... others just smiled curiously.

Every once in a while, the Ghost would bellow out again,
"I'm the ghost with THE SMELLY
OLD UNDERWEAR. BEWAAARE!"
And everyone would shout in reply…

"THEN PUT ON SOME CLEAN ONES STRAIGHT AWAY!"

And all of them, even the Ghost, laughed together.
After that, no one in Scaryville

WAS EVER SCARED AGAIN!

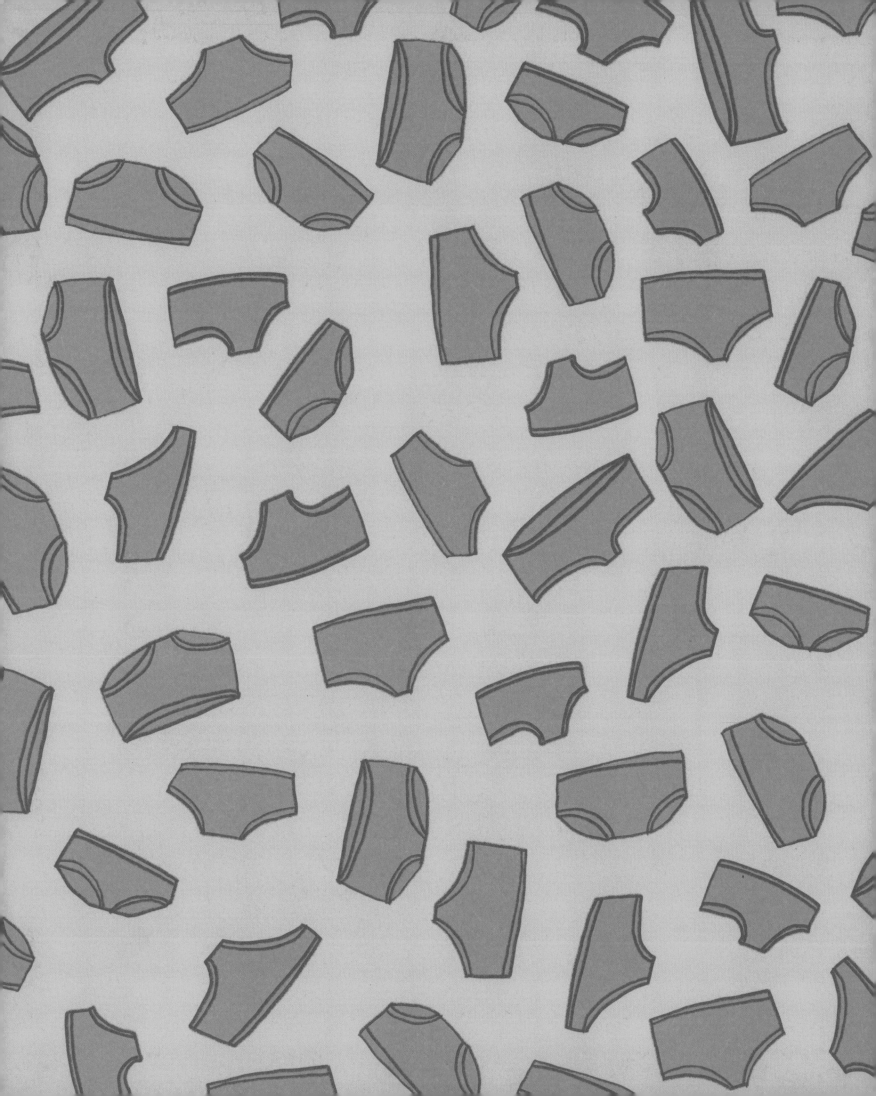